Blitz

by HETTY BURLINGAME BEATTY

Illustrated by JAMES DWYER

Front cover illustrated by Leo Sommers

SCHOLASTIC BOOK SERVICES

NEW YORK • TORONTO • LONDON • AUCKLAND • SYDNEY • TOKYO

To Lew with love

ISBN 0-590-01460-9

20 19 18 17 16 15 14 13 12   3 4 5 6 7/8

Printed in the U.S.A.   11

Contents

A Colt with
a Zigzag Streak

THEY FOUND HIM ASLEEP beside his mother the morning after he was born, and they named him Blitz because of the zigzag white marking that ran like lightning down his little nose. The early sunshine was pouring down on the green hillside, and the brook in the valley was singing its spring song as it raced along.

Blitz's mother lifted her head and nickered as Johnny and his father came across the pasture to see her new son.

"Well done, Linda girl," Johnny's father said softly, stroking her nose. "Another fine colt! You're a good mare, Linda."

5

Blitz woke up suddenly, startled by the first human voice he'd ever heard. With a terrific scramble he untangled his long wobbly legs and stood up. Seeing Johnny and his father, he gave a frightened squeal and tried to run behind his mother, but his legs went in all directions instead and he fell down in a small excited heap.

Johnny laughed delightedly, and Linda turned and nuzzled her new colt with a reassuring nicker.

So life began for Blitz on a sunny hillside in the spring, and it began with kindness from the start. Johnny came out to the pasture every day to bring

carrots and apples for Linda and to stroke Blitz's soft little nose. Blitz soon learned to look forward to these visits, and as his legs grew stronger, he went frisking across the hillside to meet Johnny.

As the months went by, Blitz grew in size and strength. He capered up and down the hillside, and his legs grew strong and straight. His woolly colt hair began to shed, and by fall the shiny red-brown of his coat glistened in the sun. His bushy little mane and tail were coal black.

When the first snowstorm came, Blitz and Linda were moved to the big barn for the winter. Johnny

led Linda down the hillside and Blitz followed, the white snowflakes whirling all around them as they went. It was the first snow Blitz had ever seen, and he loved it. He kicked up his heels and danced among the snowflakes.

Linda followed Johnny quietly through the wide barn door, but Blitz wouldn't follow. He had never been in a building before, and it looked dark and frightening inside. Linda nickered to him, but Blitz turned and ran back toward the pasture. Then he was frightened at being all alone and ran back to the barn, but still he wouldn't go in. Linda stood inside nickering to him to follow, 'and Blitz stood outside squealing with fright. Finally Johnny's big collie dog ran up behind him barking, and Blitz forgot everything and dashed into the barn to find Linda. He was trembling all over. The world was so full of new things!

So winter came, and Blitz's world changed from the free sunny hillside to the warm shadowy barn. As he grew used to it, he liked the barn too. He was just tall enough to peer over the top of the stall door and watch everything that went on.

For the first time in his life Blitz saw horses work. He saw Johnny's father harness the big gray team and drive off to the wood lot. Most amazing of all, he saw Johnny climb up on Linda's back and ride off to school, and Blitz found himself all alone in the stall. He thought they had forgotten him, and whinnied as loudly as he could. But they went away without him and didn't come back for many hours. Blitz spent the whole day running in circles around the stall, whinnying with fright and loneliness. When they finally did come, Blitz was trembling all over, but Linda only nickered softly to him as if to say, "Foolish fellow, don't you know that all horses work?"

After a few days Blitz grew used to being left alone and, after Linda and Johnny had left, Johnny's father often let Blitz follow the big gray team to the wood lot. This was much more fun than staying in the stall, and he frisked and capered around the big plodding horses as they hauled logs to the sawmill. Johnny's father always said that the best way to begin training a colt was to let it watch the older horses work. So Blitz's education began while he was very small, and being intelligent, he quickly adjusted to the ways of horses and men.

The next three and a half years were ones of growth and learning. They were happy ones for

Blitz, with moments of fright and bewilderment over new things, but always kindness and patience while he learned. The summers were spent in the hillside pasture eating the rich green grass, and the winters were times of learning for Blitz and Johnny both.

As Blitz grew into a full-grown horse, he became very handsome. His sleek red-bay coat glistened in the sun, and his black mane and tail grew long and silky. His neck was arched, his chest broad, and his legs strong and clean-cut. He was fast and powerfully built, he had quick wits for learning, and there was no streak of meanness in him anywhere. When he was three, he had already learned to pull a wagon and Johnny began riding him to school. He was a fine horse, and Johnny's father was well pleased with him.

Blitz Becomes
a Fire Horse

IN OCTOBER, the annual Fair came to a nearby town. Blitz was full grown and well trained, but he didn't know that he was to be sold. To him the farm was home, and the thought of leaving it had never occurred to him.

When Johnny and his father came to the barn on that bright October morning, Blitz whinnied happily in greeting. He watched them harness Linda to the buggy, and then Johnny led him out of his stall and fastened his lead rope to the back of it. This was something new, but Blitz was not afraid until Johnny stroked his nose gently. Suddenly a strange uneasiness came into Blitz's heart. There

11

was a sadness in Johnny; and as Blitz sensed it, a thin fear stirred in him.

Johnny was always sad when the colts were sold. He grew so fond of them. But this was the way of life, the way of a farmer who must earn his living, and Johnny would not cry before his father. When he grew up, he too would raise fine colts and sell them at the Fair.

The buggy moved off down the road with Blitz trotting close behind it, the October sun glistening on his sleek coat. The air was frosty, and Blitz tossed his head with spirit as he trotted on. The fear was gone. It must have been some foolish thing, like all his other moments of meeting a new experience for the first time. Overhead the sky was blue, and the autumn leaves made wild, gay patterns of color along the road.

It was three miles to the Fair, and soon the road became crowded with wagons, horses, and livestock of all kinds. Small flocks of woolly sheep wandered along the roadside, the sheepdogs herding them. Pigs squealed from wagons, and crates of chickens made a bedlam of cackling. Blitz shied and danced a little at the sight of these things, but it was mostly good spirits.

The fairgrounds were gay and crowded with big tents, a Ferris wheel, and stands filled with soda pop and ice cream. A brass band blared its clamorous music. Johnny and his father tied Linda to the long hitching rail and led Blitz into a little paddock filled with horses of all sorts and sizes. Again the strange fear crept into Blitz's heart, but Johnny and his father were there, so it must be all right.

As Blitz stood among the other horses, a crowd of people gradually drifted into the paddock, looking the horses over, picking out the ones they wanted to buy at the auction. Most of them stopped to look at Blitz with exclamations of admiration, and the uneasy fear clutched at his heart again as the strangers crowded around him. But Johnny spoke gently to him, and Blitz stood quietly as he'd been taught.

A man with a gruff, kind voice and gentle hands stopped when he saw Blitz and went over him carefully. He looked at the broad chest, powerful back, and strong, clean-cut legs and hoofs, and found them sound. Blitz liked his kind voice and gentle touch.

A voice shouted through the loud-speaker that the auction was about to begin, and the crowd

13

moved out to the wooden benches beside the paddock. The auctioneer took his place on the stand in front of the benches and the horses were led up beside him, one at a time. Each buyer shouted the price he was willing to pay. If someone else wanted the same horse, he shouted a higher bid, and excitement grew as the bids went higher and higher. When the top price was reached and there were no more bids, the auctioneer brought his wooden hammer down with a thud, announcing that the horse was sold. The new owner led the horse away and another horse was led up to the auctioneer's stand. Often several people wanted the same horse, and they went on shouting higher and higher bids in order to get it.

Blitz heard the shouting and saw the horses led away. He didn't understand what it was all about, but the uneasy fear crept into his heart again.

Finally it was Blitz's turn, and Johnny's father led him to the auction stand. Blitz was nervous, but he stood quietly, tossing his head and snorting a little as he looked about. Many people wanted to buy Blitz, and the bidding was long and excited. Through it all one voice rose quietly above the others, raising the bid each time. It was Sye Perkins, the gruff, kindly man. He had set his heart on buying Blitz, and he was willing to pay well for him.

As the bids went higher and higher, the other voices began to drop out. The price reached two hundred dollars and then three hundred. There was a silence, and then Sye Perkins' voice shouted, "Three hundred and fifty dollars!" There was no answer. The auctioneer waited to see if anyone would bid even higher, then he lifted his hammer over the block.

"Going — going — GONE!" he shouted. "Sold to Sye Perkins for three hundred and fifty dollars, and it looks as if you're getting a fine horse, Sye! If you don't make it first to every fire in Drumlin with that one, I'll wager it won't be the horse's fault!"

Sye laughed happily and, walking up to Blitz, stroked his nose. Then he shook hands with Johnny's father.

"Well, sir," he said, "you always did raise the best horses in the county. If Blitz is as fast as you say he is, I'll have the best team of fire horses in Drumlin for sure! Since the old mare died, I've been looking for a horse as fast and as smart as old Frank. They'll make a fine team, I think."

Johnny's father shook Sye's hand warmly. "You're

15

getting a good one all right, Sye, and I'm mighty glad Blitz is going to you. I'm always glad when my horses fall into good hands. I hate to see a horse abused."

They talked a bit while Johnny stroked Blitz's nose in silence. Then Sye took the lead rope and, with a wave and a smile, he led Blitz away.

Blitz liked this man with the kind, gruff voice, and he was glad to move away from the crowd and the shouting. When they reached the hitching rail, Blitz thought for a moment that he would be tied behind Linda's buggy again. But Sye led him past Linda to a powerfully built black horse hitched to another buggy.

"That's Frank," Sye said to Blitz, as he tied him to the back of the buggy. "You and he are going to make one mighty fine team if I'm any guesser!"

Blitz nickered nervously and looked back at Linda, who answered him from the hitching rail. Sye untied Frank and got into the buggy, and they started off down the road. Suddenly Blitz realized that he was being taken away — away from Linda, away from Johnny and his father, away from the farm and everything he'd ever known. Panic surged wildly inside him. He whinnied and whinnied, and Linda answered him.

Sye spoke gently to him. "Easy boy, easy. It's all right, boy, easy does it!"

The kind voice was reassuring, and Blitz quieted a little, though he still longed desperately to dash back to Linda and Johnny. He was strong, and he knew that if he jerked hard enough on the lead rope he could break it and be free. But deep in his brain were the lessons Johnny's father had so patiently taught him. "Never break harness, never lose your head when you're afraid, never fight back. Keep steady and try to do what you're told." The schooling had been long and sound, and Blitz steadied as he followed the buggy away from all the things he had known and loved. It must be all right somehow. Sye's voice was kind and comforting, and Frank trotted ahead of him with good spirit and no fear. Blitz took new heart and trotted down the road into his new life courageously, neck arched and head held high.

The Thrill
of the Clanging Bell

IT WAS TWELVE MILES to Drumlin. The road wandered through rolling hills and fields, then crossed long stretches of salt marsh, and the sharp smell of the sea struck Blitz's nostrils for the first time.

They crossed a bridge and came into a new country that was to be Blitz's home. Hills, woods, and great granite ledges ran down to the sea that surrounded it. It was a land of rockbound farms, quarries, and scattered villages. The road followed the edge of the sea for several miles and finally reached Drumlin, with its snug harbors and sturdy fishing boats. The sun was low in the west when they turned into a narrow road leading to a farm tucked among the wild ledges and scrub pine.

Frank pulled the buggy through the wide door and stopped in the shadowy warmth of the barn. Blitz was tired and hungry after the long journey, and the smell of good hay made him nicker softly. Sye unharnessed Frank, unfastened Blitz's lead rope, and led them both to the watering trough for a cool drink. Then he led them into their stalls, bedded with fresh, clean straw, and gave them both a good feed of oats and hay. Blitz nickered hungrily as he munched his oats. Sye kept talking in his kind, gruff voice, and he gave them both an affectionate slap on the rump as he left to get his own supper.

"Just wait till old Bob Rogers sees the team I've got now!" he muttered happily as he went out the barn door.

For a little while Blitz missed his old home. Above all he missed Johnny, but Sye's grandchildren brought him apples and carrots after school, and Frank was good company.

The day after Blitz's arrival, Sye harnessed him with Frank to a work wagon and they hauled firewood to the village. It took a long time, because Sye had to stop every other minute to chat with friends. Blitz soon realized that he was the center of interest. He was looked over from end to end a hundred times on the way down Main Street. There was much head shaking and chuckling, and Sye sounded mighty pleased with himself.

On the way home, to Blitz's amazement and delight, Sye urged Frank and Blitz into a gallop, wagon and all. Frank didn't need any urging, but Blitz was confused at first. He'd been taught never to gallop in harness, much as he'd wanted to sometimes. He started up slowly and hesitantly, but when he heard Sye urging him on, he stretched his legs to the utmost and really let go.

They tore down the road, their hoofs pounding like thunder, and great clouds of dust rolling out behind the wagon. It was more fun than Blitz had ever had. At the road to the farm, Sye's strong grip on the reins pulled them into the turn without even slowing down. They thundered up to the barn, and stopped.

The next day Sye tried them out at the gallop with a heavily loaded wagon. Blitz found they could go even faster, because the wagon held the road firmly instead of bouncing and clattering behind them. Sye tried them out on narrow roads and sharp turns, and Blitz learned quickly. Then Sye took them to the Fire Station and gave them a trial run with the big pump engine! Blitz stood quietly while Sye harnessed them to it with a speed Blitz had never seen before.

Sye climbed up into the driver's seat, and a great bell clanged suddenly right behind Blitz's heels. He shot out of the door as if the devil himself were behind him, and almost missed the sharp turn into the street in his fright. Frank reached over and gave him an angry nip for his clumsiness, and Sye shouted and hauled on the reins. They made the turn somehow, and swung into the long, straight street which was crowded with cheering people.

Blitz lost his head a bit. The wild clanging bell behind him put panic in his heart. No wagon he'd ever pulled in his life had made noises like this one! He stretched out his neck and tore down the street wildly. Frank raced beside him at a pounding gallop, but gradually Blitz realized that Frank was not running because he was afraid. His gallop was steady and controlled, and he reached over and nipped Blitz impatiently as he ran. They ran for two miles before the fear began to leave Blitz's pounding heart, and his gallop steadied to an even pace beside Frank. Sye didn't try to stop Blitz until he saw that he was steadying down, for he knew that the best way to handle a strong horse is to let him run his fear out.

When Sye finally pulled them to a stop, Frank laid back his ears and snapped angrily again at Blitz's neck. It was very evident that Frank was telling him in no uncertain terms what he thought of him! Sye laughed and watched Frank driving the lesson home.

"Attaboy, Frank," he shouted. "You tell him what's what and why. He'll understand you better than he does me!"

Blitz did understand. Frank left no room for doubt in his mind! When Sye gathered up the reins again and swung the engine toward home, Blitz moved quietly and turned carefully and quickly. When the bell started clanging, Blitz quivered all over and was about to set off again, but a quick snap from Frank reminded him.

Sye eased them into a slow gallop on the road

home, and by the time they reached the Fire Station Blitz was no longer afraid of the bell. He soon learned to love the exciting clanging as much as Frank did.

Sye rested them for a while, and then did a practice run through the village to give Blitz some experience. They did sharp turns, quick stops, and swings into narrow roads and driveways. Blitz was always quick to learn and, with Frank and Sye guiding him, he was handling the engine like an old-timer when Sye swung them back to the Fire Station again.

"Good work, boys," Sye said, as he climbed down from the engine and stroked both their noses proudly with his rough, gnarled hand.

Sye drove them home slowly. They were sweating from the long workout, and he wanted them to cool off gradually, so they wouldn't get stiff. Blitz was mighty glad to see his stall and a good feed that night. He was tired, but he was already happy in his new life. He loved Sye, and all the children patted him and brought him things to eat. Above all, the thrill of that fast run with the fire engine had struck a deep spark in his heart. All his life Blitz had loved to run at top speed, stretching his strong legs and muscles. In this job he really could!

As he slept, he dreamed of the clanging engine and the wild dash down the road, and he nickered happily in his dreams. The fear was gone, and the gallant heart of a fire horse was born within him.

Blitz Lives
Up to His Name

LIKE MOST SMALL TOWNS, Drumlin had a volunteer Fire Department. The fire engines were owned by the town and kept in the town Fire Station, but the horses that pulled them were owned by local farmers. The fastest team got to the Fire Station first, although it also depended on whose team happened to be nearest when the fire alarm blew. There was always keen competition between the fastest teams.

Drumlin had three fire engines. The chemical wagon always went out first, carrying chemical extinguishers and long lines of fire hose. Half the crew held the fire at bay with the chemicals while the other half laid the hose line to the nearest water supply. In those days only the center of the town had hydrants, and water often had to be pumped from wells or quarry ponds.

The pump engine carried the steam boiler and pump. While it was on its way, the firemen stoked the fire in the boiler, making steam to run the pump when they got there. The pump engine always went out second, to pump water to the fire as soon as the hose was laid.

The hook and ladder went out last, bringing the ladders for climbing roofs and rescuing people from top floors. All the engines were painted glistening red and gold, and the town was very proud of them.

Sye Perkins always tried to get to the Fire Station first, take the chemical wagon, and arrive first at every fire. For years he and Bob Rogers had competed in this. Bob Rogers' team was fast, but they were heavier built than Sye's and they often got left with the pump instead.

Andy Johnson and Joe Woodbury competed for the hook and ladder. Ben Jones had the fifth team. They were good horses, but not as fast as the others, and Ben only made it if he was very close to the Fire Station when the alarm blew.

When Bob Rogers first saw Blitz, his heart sank. Sye's old mare had been fast, and nobody could beat Frank, but Bob shook his head when he looked over the clean, strong lines of Blitz's legs and body. He knew horseflesh well and, to his reckoning, Blitz spelled speed! When he saw him on a first trial run, stretched out neck and neck with old Frank, Bob had a fair hunch that he was licked for good on first place. He scratched his beard glumly, and Sye chuckled with a happy glint in his eye.

Two days after Blitz's first experience with the fire engine, he and Frank were hauling a heavy load of gravel near the edge of the town. Suddenly the fire alarm blew. Blitz had never heard it before, but Frank was quivering with excitement at the first blast of the whistle. The load was too heavy for speed, and Sye jumped off the wagon and unhitched the team. He leaped on Frank's back, and both horses plunged into a gallop as the whistle went on shrieking the call for a fire on the North Road two miles out.

They tore into the engine house, and Sye had

them hitched to the chemical wagon in less time than it takes to tell it. The volunteer crew were running from all directions. Six of them jumped onto the chemical wagon as Sye leaped into the driver's seat and took up the reins. Frank and Blitz charged out the door, the bell clanging behind them. For a moment Blitz almost lost his head again in the excitement, but halfway out the door he remembered his earlier lesson. He gathered his strong haunches under him to make the sharp turn into the street, and the chemical wagon swung smoothly behind them. Then they were off!

First there were the sharp turns through the village, then the open road stretched out before them and both horses swung into their fastest gallop. The engine flew along behind them, its bell clanging wildly. The whole town turned out to follow, and in a few minutes the road was crowded with horses, buggies, and wagons.

As they reached a bend in the road, they saw a column of smoke rising from the Erkolas' farmhouse. Sye hauled on the reins to slow his team for the sharp turn into the farm road, but Frank had already spotted the smoke and knew where they were going. Blitz tried to do as Frank did, and they made the turn shoulder to shoulder and raced up the hill to the farm. They had hardly stopped when the crew jumped off, hauling the hose line to the well while three of the firemen dashed into the house with the chemical extinguishers.

The Erkola chimney was old, and a hot wood fire in the kitchen range had sent sparks through a crack into the hollow of the wall. It had been smoldering since early morning and suddenly had burst into flames, burning through the back wall of the house. A neighbor saw it and sent in the alarm. When Mrs. Erkola heard the alarm blow, she ran outside to see where the fire was, and to her horror found it was her own house! Her husband had gone to town to get the mower fixed, but the neighbors ran to help with buckets of water. Before the first buckets were filled, the chemical engine raced clanging into the yard.

The hose line was hardly laid when Bob Rogers swung the heavy pump engine up beside it, and the hose was quickly coupled to the pump. In a matter of minutes a stream of water was pouring into the flaming hole in the back of the house.

The ladder truck followed with Andy Johnson's team. They'd beaten Joe Woodbury again, and there was a smug look of pleasure on Andy's face as his crew lifted a ladder and ran for the back of the house. As soon as the ladder was in place, two firemen ran up it with axes and chopped a larger hole, so the water could reach the fire inside the wall.

The fire was out after twenty minutes of hard work and water. The house was saved, and not much damage was done except for a charred, jagged hole in the back wall and some plaster spoiled by the deluge of water. The crowd cheered enthusiastically. But for the speed of Drumlin's Fire Department, the whole house would have burned to the ground!

It took a little while to uncouple the hose line and load it back into the chemical wagon. It also took a bit of time to discuss the fire, and Sye and Bob had to have their usual banter about whose horses were the faster. When it was over, Sye climbed back into the driver's seat with a wide grin on his face.

"Good boys," he said, as he turned Frank and Blitz and headed for the main road. "Good boy, Blitz," he added. "You'll be as good as Frank in no time at all at the rate you're going!"

Blitz heard the praise in Sye's voice and tossed his head with pride. Sye took them back to the Fire Station at a slow gallop, unhitched them, and headed back with them to his load of gravel.

Blitz had been to his first fire, and the farm wagon was dull by comparison; but there was a prouder arch in his neck as he pulled it. After that, Blitz's ears were constantly on the alert for the fire alarm.

First to the Fire

WHEN WINTER SET IN, Sye had the blacksmith put sharp pegs on the horses' shoes to keep them from slipping on the icy roads. In cold weather most of the fires were caused by overheated stoves and old, cracked chimneys, but in January there was a bad fire which no one could explain.

Ray Mathews, a newcomer in Drumlin, had bought a building on Main Street a few months before. There were two shops on the street floor, and a fair-sized apartment upstairs over them. All three were occupied and bringing in a good rent each month. The Drumlin townspeople were always a bit standoffish with strangers, but Ray took such an interest in the town that everyone grew to like him. He seemed to be a smart businessman, which impressed people, and he enthusiastically backed all the town's improvement efforts. He joined the volunteer Fire Department as soon as he arrived in Drumlin, and he seemed to be a very public-spirited man.

The building on Main Street which Ray had bought was in good repair. The chimneys were sound and the stoves were almost new. When the building suddenly burst into flames at one o'clock on a January morning, everyone was puzzled about the cause.

Blitz and Frank were dozing in the warm barn when the fire alarm blew, but they were wide awake and prancing with impatience to be off before the first blast had ended. Sye came running out to the barn, pulling on his clothes as he ran. As Blitz's stall was nearer, Sye harnessed him first. Blitz was dancing with excitement and, while Sye harnessed Frank, he backed out of the stall by himself and stood waiting by the open barn door.

The fire whistle was still blowing the alarm. Over and over its shrill blast tore through the night air, shattering the peaceful silence of the little village with its warning sound. Blitz hesitated a moment, but the call of the whistle was too much for him. He shot out the door at a gallop and headed for the Fire Station all alone, his harness flapping as he ran.

When Blitz reached the Fire Station, he found most of the volunteer firemen already there waiting for the horses. Blitz charged through the doorway, nearly knocking them down in his rush. Taken by surprise, and seeing him with no driver or teammate, the half-awake firemen angrily shooed him out the door. Blitz was confused and a little frightened. He'd never been out dashing about in the night by himself, and he'd evidently done the wrong thing. He swung around and headed for home. Halfway there, he met Frank tearing down the road toward the Fire Station with Sye on his back. Sye shouted to him, and Blitz turned in midstride and fell in beside Frank at the dead gallop. Sye was laughing as he clung to Frank's back.

"What's the matter?" he shouted at Blitz. "Are Frank and I getting too slow for you these days? It's a wonder you didn't drag the fire engine off with your teeth before we got there!"

Blitz tossed his head happily as he ran. He heard

the pride and affection in Sye's voice, and he knew that Sye was pleased and amused by his impatient dash to the Fire Station by himself.

In less than three minutes Blitz and Frank were swinging the chemical wagon into Main Street. The blazing building lit up the whole street, and clouds of black smoke rolled out over the sea in the night wind. A crowd had already gathered, and people were running in and out of the building, dragging out everything they could carry. The street was piled with furniture and stock from the two stores.

The hose was coupled to the Main Street hydrant as the pump engine clattered to a stop, and the hook and ladder clanged up behind it. This was the worst fire Blitz had ever seen. The whole Fire Department was needed, and most of the bystanders pitched in to help. Ladders were thrown up against the front of the building, and the hose played through the blazing windows into the heart of the fire. For three hours the firemen battled the raging flames before the "all out" whistle blew its two shrill blasts. The building was still partly standing, but it was charred and black and completely burned out inside. It was a total loss.

No one knew how the fire had started, but everyone felt sorry for Ray Mathews. He'd been among the first to get to the engine house, and he had fought as hard as anyone to check the fire. His face was smeared with soot, and his clothes were torn and scorched.

When the fire was out, Blitz and Frank swung the chemical wagon back to the Fire Station. Sye unhitched them and headed for home, holding the horses to a walk. He seemed tired and in no mood to hurry. As they clopped along the road, Sye talked half to himself and half to his horses.

"Funny how that fire got going," he muttered. "If we had one of those newfangled motor pumps they tell about, I'll bet we could have saved that building! I'm not for motorized engines instead of horses, 'cause you can't count on them newfangled things, but they say those motor pumps can sure do a job of pumping water once you get there."

Sye scratched his head as he jogged along. The only thing that ever really got Sye down was losing a fight with a fire. He hated to see a good building destroyed, and he felt sorry for the owners who lost it. It was this spirit in the Drumlin Fire Department that made its members keep trying to think up better ways of fighting fires and faster ways of getting there in time.

Through the rest of that winter there were several fires in the town. No week went by without at least one, but most of them were stopped in time. One barn, far out from the town, burned to the ground, but in every other case the Drumlin Fire Department was so quick that the fire was put out before much damage was done. The town was well pleased with its firemen and also with its fire horses. Blitz and Frank were rapidly becoming famous for their speed and skill, and several other larger towns tried to buy them. But Sye turned down every offer, no matter how big it was. He had no intention of parting with his famous team.

In the spring, Ray Mathews collected the insurance for his burned-out building on Main Street. Everyone in Drumlin was glad to find that it was well covered by insurance, and that he was paid quite a bit more than the building had cost him. No loss after all! Both the insurance company and the State Police investigated to see if someone had set the fire, but they found no clues. The cause of the fire remained a complete mystery.

Ray took the insurance money and bought a summer hotel near the sea. He called it the Sea House and opened up for business that June. The former owner had managed it badly and the business had failed. Because of this, Ray was able to buy it at a low price. Ray was obviously a smart businessman, and it looked as if he would make a good thing of his summer hotel.

A Midnight Tragedy

IN FEBRUARY of that same winter, a new volunteer member joined the Drumlin Fire Department. No one knew where he came from or even what his name was.

Sye was riding his team home from a fire when he noticed a stray dog following the horses. He looked at it with curiosity because he'd never seen it before and didn't know where it had come from. It was a coach dog, white with neat round black spots all over it. It followed close behind Blitz's heels, and when they reached the barn it trotted inside and sat down near the door. Sye paid little attention to the dog while he unharnessed Blitz and

Frank and fed them, thinking it must have strayed from a neighboring town and would go home by itself.

When Sye was ready to close the barn door, he called the dog outside. The night was bitterly cold, and the dog stood shivering in the dim light of Sye's lantern. Sye was always soft-hearted about animals, and he hated to think of the dog out in the cold all night. It looked hungry as well as cold, and Sye ended by going into the house and getting a bowl of scraps. He let the dog inside the warm barn to eat them.

"You can stay there tonight, feller," he said, "but in the morning you go home to wherever you came from. Understand?"

The dog wagged its tail and whined softly as it dove hungrily into the bowl of scraps. Sye closed the barn door and headed for the house.

In the morning the dog was curled up on the straw in Blitz's stall. When Sye hitched the team and started for town with a load of stove wood, the dog followed them. Sye kept telling it to go home, but the dog just wagged its tail and kept following.

That afternoon the fire whistle blew again. The fire was on East Main Street and, as usual, Blitz and

Frank were the first to get there. It wasn't till the fire was out that Sye noticed that the dog was still with them.

"Anybody know where that spotted dog came from?" he asked of the gathered crowd.

No one knew. In fact no one had even noticed the dog till Sye spoke of it.

After that the dog lived in the barn with Blitz and Frank, and Sye fed it. If it had a home, it never went back to it; and it wasn't long before Sye noticed that the dog loved the Fire Department as much as Blitz and Frank did. All day it followed the team, but when the fire whistle blew, it went wild with excitement. It ran in circles around Blitz and Frank, barking, and then dashed off ahead of them to the Fire Station. When the chemical wagon raced out at the gallop, the dog raced with it.

The dog soon became the mascot of the Drumlin Fire Department and always went with Sye and the chemical engine. Just once Sye missed getting to the Fire Station first. He was far out on the South Road when the fire whistle blew, and Bob Rogers was hauling coal on Main Street. Bob got there first.

Blitz and Frank galloped their fastest to get there, but the dog raced ahead and outdistanced them.

As Sye clattered up to the engine house, the chemical wagon charged out with Bob Rogers in the driver's seat. The dog was following it and paid no attention to Blitz and Frank, who were left to pull the pump engine. When the fire was out, Bob Rogers turned to Sye with a malicious grin.

"What's the matter, Sye?" he laughed. "Are those horses of yours getting old, or did you put lead in their shoes? Even the dog beat them to the fire!"

Sye mumbled something under his breath that probably wasn't fit to say out loud. Sure enough, the dog had beaten them to the fire, and to make it worse, he walked up to Sye and gave him an unmistakable look of reproach. Everyone laughed.

"Sye, it isn't you and your horses that dog cares about," one of the firemen said, "it's getting to the fire first! I vote we elect him an official member of the Drumlin Fire Department, and that we name him Chief because he's always first at every fire!"

There was a roar of laughter and cheers from the crowd. So Chief was named and became an official member of the Drumlin Fire Department.

Life went on in Drumlin as it always had. Work to be done, loads to be hauled, days begun and days ended. But for Blitz and Frank and Chief the sound of the fire whistle was the one important thing. It blew often enough to keep them good and busy. When the winter was over, the grass fires began, but Drumlin still held the best record of any town in the county for putting its fires out fast.

Blitz was no longer a raw colt, but an expert and keenly intelligent fire horse. As the months went on, the combination of hard work, good feed, and fast runs filled out his muscles and broadened his strong chest. His red-bay coat glistened from Sye's daily brushings, and his neck arched proudly. Blitz was the pride of the whole town.

Then one September night the screeching blast of the fire whistle blew at midnight. The whole town was awake and dressed by the time it had blown its third round. The fire must be a big one!

Sye raced for the barn, pulling on his clothes as he went. Chief dashed out the door and headed for the Fire Station, waiting for no one. Blitz and Frank were prancing impatiently as Sye harnessed them.

When they charged out the barn door a minute later, with Sye on Blitz's back, the whole sky to the north was aglow. Sye leaned low over Blitz's neck and urged him on.

"This must be a big one, boys," he shouted to his

team as they thundered down to the Fire Station.
It was! It was Ray Mathews' hotel.

As the chemical wagon raced up the hill, Chief
was in the lead, and Blitz and Frank were stretched
out neck and neck, faster than they had ever run.
Sye was standing in the driver's seat, shouting to
them for more and more speed. They could see the
flames roaring through the roof of the hotel and
piling up in a flaming pyramid against the sky.

Just before the hotel there was a sharp bend in
the road. Blitz and Frank knew it well, and so did
Sye. They didn't even slow down for the turn. On
they went at a thundering gallop.

Then it happened! There in the road before them was a great log, a whole section of tree trunk ready to be sawed. It lay across the road at a casual angle as if it might have fallen from a wagon. Blitz and Frank saw it before Sye did. Without breaking stride they leaped over it, but the right front wheel of the chemical wagon hit it head on. The fire engine veered with a wrench that threw both horses off the road and tossed Sye out of the driver's seat. There was a sickening crash, then silence!

The End of
the Fire Fighters

THE OTHER FIRE ENGINES raced past the wreck, swerving to the left to miss the tree trunk which had been swung partly off the road by the impact of the chemical wagon. Then followed the buggies, the chugging cars, and the running people from the town.

It was easy to see that Ray Mathews' hotel was past saving. The season was over and the hotel closed, so there was no need to rescue anyone. Nothing to do but let it burn and keep the fire from spreading to other houses. The pump and hook-and-ladder crews tackled that, while the rest of the crowd ran back to the wrecked chemical wagon.

Sye and the five firemen who had been on it were unconscious. Frank, the loyal old fire horse, was dead. His head had struck a tree, killing him instantly. Blitz was lying in the ditch, pinned down by the wreckage of the chemical wagon. Chief was standing beside him whining and shivering.

Old Doc Jones climbed out of his Ford and ran to Sye, who was badly hurt. The other firemen had only been knocked out and came to in a few minutes, so Doc Jones turned all his attention to Sye. They lifted him gently into the doctor's car and carried him off to the hospital in the next town.

Then the crowd turned to the horses. When they saw that good old Frank was dead, they turned to Blitz and began pulling the wreckage off him. When he was free, Blitz staggered to his feet and stood there trembling. His back ached with a searing pain that made him weak all over.

The crowd went back to the fire to help save the neighboring houses, leaving Blitz alone with Billy Erkola. Billy stroked his nose gently and felt him all over for broken bones. There didn't seem to be any. He was just terribly wrenched and strained and bruised. Billy spoke soothingly to him as he led him out into the road.

Blitz could hardly walk. As Billy led him down the hill toward home, he didn't look much like the strong, spirited horse that had charged up it at the dead gallop a few minutes before. Billy led him slowly, and Blitz stumbled along beside him.

When they reached Sye's barn, Billy led him into his stall and gave him a feed of oats, but Blitz wasn't hungry. He was still in a daze, and he ached from end to end. In a vague, confused way he realized that Frank was dead and that Sye had been carried off silent and still. A cold numbness settled over him as Billy went out and closed the door, leaving him alone in the dark silent barn. Even Chief wasn't there to comfort him.

Chief was still at the fire. He had stayed by the wreck at first, sniffing of Sye and Frank and Blitz and whimpering softly. Then he walked over to the log that had caused the wreck, sniffing it with interest. After that, he wandered back to the crowd by the fire.

The heat from the fire was so terrific that it had singed most of the hair off one of Bob Rogers' horses. The whole building was a roaring mass of flame rising into the spark-filled sky. The firemen battled furiously to keep the fire from spreading.

When the roof caved in, a great volcano of sparks rose and scattered, starting several small fires. But quick work put them out, and the nearby houses were saved. Finally there was nothing left of the hotel but a mass of glowing embers. The crowd watched in silence as the pump engine went on pouring water on the smoldering ruins. Then they wandered back again to the wrecked chemical wagon. Ray Mathews was with the crowd, and everyone was feeling sorry for him. It seemed that bad luck was following him. First his building on Main Street had burned, and now his hotel was gone.

The wreck was a sad sight. The chemical wagon was completely smashed, and old Frank still lay where he had fallen. The men looked the wreck over, then turned to the log that had caused it, wondering how it got in the road. If it had fallen off a wagon in the daytime, surely someone would have noticed it before dark, and it hardly seemed possible that anything as big as that could have fallen off a wagon without the driver's knowing it. The men discussed it and were deeply puzzled.

Suddenly Ray Mathews stepped forward, his face white and angry under the black smears of soot. No one had ever seen Ray Mathews really angry before.

"That Sye Perkins was speed-mad!" he shouted angrily. "All he ever cared about was showing off how fast those horses of his could go. Always driving like crazy to every fire! It's a wonder he never got wrecked before. Serves him right, I say!"

The crowd was deeply shocked by Ray's angry tirade. Everyone loved Sye Perkins and his horses. Sye had no enemies in Drumlin, only friends who knew him well and loved him. There was a strained silence for a moment; then a strange thing happened. Chief walked over to the log and sniffed it carefully again. Then he walked over to Ray Mathews and sniffed him. Slowly the hair rose on his back, and he drew back his lips in a low snarling growl. Ray jumped back, kicking at Chief.

"Get that ugly cur out of here!" he shouted. "There's been enough trouble tonight without that brute biting me into the bargain!"

For a moment the crowd was sympathetic, thinking Ray was just badly upset by the loss of his hotel. It was enough to upset anyone! But it wasn't like Chief to snarl at people.

Slowly and grimly an idea dawned in Bob Rogers' mind. Without saying a word, he took a lantern from one of the bystanders and walked into the woods at the edge of the road. The crowd watched him go, in puzzled silence. They heard his heavy boots tramping through the underbrush, then an excited shout. Following him into the woods, they found him standing beside the stump of a tree, thirty feet from the road. The stump was so freshly cut that sap was still oozing out and trickling down its sides. There was a trampled area around it, and the leaves on the chopped-off treetop were still fresh and green. A torn groove in the earth showed where the heavy log had been dragged out to the road. Someone had caused the wreck on purpose! Who? And why?

When the men returned to the road, Ray had vanished. It didn't take long to get the facts and piece the story together from there. The insurance company reported that Ray had insured the hotel for ten thousand dollars more than he had paid for it, on the grounds that he was making extensive improvements in the building. The improvements had not been made, except for a paint job which had cost only a few hundred dollars.

The case looked pretty clear against Ray Mathews. When the State Police caught him a few days later in a distant town, he finally confessed that he had set both fires and had dragged the log into the road to keep the fire engines from reaching the hotel fire in time. He was sent to prison for a long term for setting the fires; and if Sye Perkins had died, he would have been charged with murder, too!

But Sye Perkins didn't die. Both legs were broken and he was badly hurt all over. He would live, but Doc Jones said he would never be able to drive a fire engine again or do heavy work. He lay for many weeks in the hospital before he could even sit up in a wheel chair. It would be many months before Sye would walk again.

The Town Board of Drumlin held a meeting the day after the accident, to decide how to replace the wrecked chemical wagon. After long discussion, it was voted to buy one of the new motorized fire trucks. It was the beginning of the end of the days of horse-drawn fire engines in Drumlin; and when the new fire engine arrived, the whole town turned out to celebrate its arrival.

Blitz Goes to the City

Blitz stood alone in his stall, his wrenched body racked with pain and his legs stiff and swollen. Billy Erkola came to feed and water him and rub his aching joints with liniment, and Sye's wife and grandchildren brought him tidbits and tried to comfort him in his pain and loneliness.

Chief had moved permanently to the Fire Station; and when the new chemical engine arrived, he adopted it as his. It was too fast for him to run beside, so he rode in honor on the seat beside the driver. No one had forgotten that it was Chief who had helped solve the mystery of the wrecked fire engine and bring Ray Mathews to justice.

53

Sye Perkins' wife spent most of each day at the hospital with her husband. They talked often of Blitz, hoping that he would recover. Sye wanted terribly to keep him and at least assure him of a good home for the rest of his life, but the hospital expenses were very high and they needed money badly. Sadly, they decided that Blitz must be sold.

At the end of a few weeks, Sye's wife called the veterinary to look Blitz over again. He led him out of his stall and examined him carefully. When he had finished, he shook his head.

"A very long rest might do the job," he said, "but I'm afraid he'll only be good for light work at best. There's nothing broken, but he's so badly wrenched it will take a long, long time to heal. He'll be all right for light loads, I think, but nothing more."

Sye hoped that someone in Drumlin would buy Blitz and give him easy work and good care, but no one there needed a horse that couldn't pull heavy loads. There was nothing to do but try to sell him at the Fair.

Sye was still in the hospital when the Fair came, and Billy Erkola's father offered to take him to the auction. He tied Blitz to the back of his buggy, and Sye's wife came out to the barn to say good-bye to him. She was crying as Blitz followed Erkola's buggy off down the road.

It was a long, slow journey for Blitz this time. He could only trot slowly at best, and by the time they reached the fairgrounds his legs and back were stiff and aching again. The Fair was as gay as ever with laughing crowds, but Blitz didn't notice the gaiety as old man Erkola led him into the auction paddock. He ached with fatigue from the twelve-mile journey, and his heart was numb with dread at leaving Drumlin, Sye Perkins, and the life he had loved. He sensed, as animals often do, that he was not going back.

In the auction paddock, Blitz stood quietly beside old man Erkola, glad of the chance to rest his tired muscles. Several people stopped to look him over. As both Erkola and Sye Perkins were honest men, Erkola told them frankly that Blitz had been wrenched in an accident and would only be good for light work. The possible buyers turned away, looking for a sounder horse.

Then a thin, raggedly dressed man came along. He looked Blitz over and asked a few questions about him. Instead of turning away when Erkola told him about the accident, he looked interested.

"He'll be going cheap then," the man said. "You can't get much for a wrenched-up horse that can't do much. If I can get him cheap enough, I have just the job for him — a light flower wagon to pull in the city streets, and plenty of rest while I stand by the curb selling flowers. Just the thing for him, but I can't pay much."

There was something about the man that Erkola didn't like, but the work sounded easy and the man seemed sympathetic about Blitz's accident, in an unconvincing sort of way. As far as the price went, Erkola could understand a man looking for a horse that didn't cost too much, but something in the man's manner made him wonder if he would be kind to Blitz. He even tried to discourage the man's interest in buying him. Blitz felt the same way. No one had ever treated him badly in his life, yet he felt a vague fear and distrust of this man.

The auction proceeded, and when Blitz was led forward the bids were few and low. The highest bid was fifty dollars and no one raised it. The auctioneer's hammer finally fell and Blitz was sold. His new owner came forward out of the crowd to claim him. It was the ragged thin man of the flower wagon. Erkola was sorry, but there was nothing he

could do but hope he was wrong about the man, and that Blitz would have a good home and easy work after all. Joe Botts paid the fifty dollars and, taking Blitz's lead rope from Erkola, he led him out of the paddock and off down the road from the Fair.

Joe's last horse had died in the city streets three days before. Joe had been standing on the sidewalk selling flowers, and suddenly the old mare had fallen down where she stood. Joe had kicked her to make her get up, but the old mare was dead and Joe was without a horse. He had walked the five miles from the edge of the city to the Fair to buy a new one.

Blitz followed him quietly down the road. It was good to walk slowly at least. At the edge of the city Joe turned off into a lane crowded with tumble-down shacks. He turned in at one of them and led Blitz into a shabby shed behind it. It had one tiny window, and the reek of manure and moldy hay struck Blitz's nose as he went in. The straw on the dirt floor was wet and evidently hadn't been changed for months. Joe tied Blitz to a ring in the wall in one corner, threw a small armful of moldy hay down beside him, and went out without a word or a pat.

The next day was Sunday, and Blitz stood alone in the damp, dirty shed all day. Joe came out once and gave him a pailful of water and another armful of moldy hay, but Blitz hadn't finished what had been given him the night before. He couldn't choke it down, although he was very hungry.

"You'll eat it when you get hungry enough," Joe laughed harshly. "This ain't the Ritz, you know. Hard enough to buy horse food as it is!"

Blitz heard some boys playing outside, and for a moment a little spark of warmth and hope came into his heart, but it didn't last long. One boy stuck his head inside the shed.

"Look a' the plug Dad's got now," he sneered from the doorway. The others peered over his shoulder, and one of them picked up a stone and threw it at Blitz. Blitz jumped when it hit him, and the boys laughed. More stones followed, and more laughter. Then Blitz heard Joe's angry voice shouting at them, and they ran away. After that, they didn't come near the shed again.

The next morning Joe harnessed Blitz to the rickety flower wagon that stood in the yard. It wasn't heavy, and Blitz started off at an easy walk. When they turned into the main road, Joe cracked his whip sharply across Blitz's flanks. Blitz jumped and swung into a trot. He had never been whipped before, for he was more than willing to do his best, and a word was all he had ever needed. His hoofs pounded on the hard pavement, every step jarring his wrenched back and stiff legs.

Joe was quite pleased with Blitz. Even with his stiff legs he looked like a good horse, sleek and well built. In fact, Joe was so anxious to show him off that he held him at a fast trot all the way.

Hard Times

A MILE FROM JOE'S SHACK they stopped at the greenhouse where Joe bought the flowers he sold in the city. The greenhouse raised fine flowers to sell to expensive florist shops, but every day there were flowers left over which were already cut. The first day these were sold to second-rate shops, and the second day they were sold to even cheaper shops. But when the flowers were just ready to wilt, they were sold to Joe for next to nothing. They still looked quite nice, but would only last a day at best.

Joe loaded his wagon and drove into the city. The

wagon looked very gay and he usually sold most of the flowers, making just enough to feed his wife and seven children after a fashion.

The wagon wasn't heavy even when it was loaded, and Blitz trotted as fast as he could, despite the hard paving of the streets. By the end of the first day he ached in every bone and muscle, and was glad to get back to the dirty shed where he could rest. He kept shifting his weight from one aching leg to another, to ease the throbbing. He was terribly hungry from the day's work, and he choked down the moldy hay Joe had given him.

During the night it rained. The shed roof leaked badly, drenching Blitz and the dirty straw he was standing on. By morning he was so stiff he could hardly move, and when Joe harnessed him to the wagon, Blitz started off at a slow, limping walk. Joe thought it laziness and lashed him with the whip.

"You did all right yesterday, you lazy brute," he shouted. "No use playing lame today!"

The whip bit into Blitz's tender flanks. Never in his life had he held back from work and, in spite of his aching legs and back, he did his best to trot. He stumbled often, and Joe jerked the reins to pull him back on his feet, bringing the whip down harder to punish him and drive him on.

Joe was bitterly disappointed in his new horse. Yesterday he had trotted into the city at a good clip, and many people had admired him. Today Blitz was lame and stiff and stumbling and slow. Joe was angry and felt cheated.

"I'll teach him he can't get away with lazy stubbornness," Joe muttered to himself, bringing the whip down viciously.

From that moment Blitz's life became a long nightmare of whiplashes, hard paved streets, and moldy hay. The pain in his back and legs grew steadily worse, but the lonely, bewildered pain in his heart was even harder to bear. All his life Blitz had known kindness and love, and had done his work well, with good spirit. Now, because he was lame and sick, he got only curses and the whip. Blitz was utterly bewildered, and slowly his gallant spirit began to break.

The harder Blitz tried and the sicker he got, the more often the lash of the whip bit into his hurting sides. His heart began to shrivel under the deluge of hate and pain and, as the months went on, starvation was added. He choked down the wisps of spoiled hay hungrily, but there wasn't enough even of that. His ribs began to show, and his dirty unbrushed coat turned dull and ragged.

Then came the ice and snow and cold of winter. At night Blitz shivered in the draughty shed, and in the daytime he struggled to keep his footing on the icy streets. Joe couldn't spare good money to put sharp pegs on his horse's shoes. It was too cold to sell flowers in winter, so Joe collected junk from back yards in the city and sold it to junk dealers. The loads were often heavy with stacks of newspapers and old iron stoves. Blitz could hardly pull them.

It was in a sleet storm that Blitz fell, pulling a heavy load up the hill near the junk yard. Joe shouted at him, jerking the reins and bringing the lash down on his back. Blitz struggled to get up, but his hoofs slid on the ice and he couldn't get a foothold.

"Get up, you lazy brute!" Joe shouted, and the lash of the whip fell again and again.

Blitz went on trying to get up, but it was no use. Then Joe completely lost his head with anger and,

jumping down off the wagon, he stood in the street lashing Blitz with every ounce of strength he had.

Blitz struggled until he was completely exhausted, then he lay still and let the whip fall. There was nothing he could do to get up or to stop the whip.

Joe was cold and tired himself, and his ragged overcoat was poor protection against the wind and sleet. It was the last straw to have Blitz fall at the end of a long day and just lie there, refusing to get up! In his anger, Joe kicked him to make him struggle harder. Blitz cringed with pain and made one more desperate effort to get his feet under him. It was useless, and he lay still again, the shafts of the heavily loaded wagon holding him down. Joe was still kicking him in useless anger when a man came down the street and stopped to watch.

"Hey!" he shouted, "you can't get him up that way. Hold on a minute and I'll help you."

"He's just a lazy brute!" Joe shouted back.

"Maybe so," the man answered, "but even if he is, you'll never get him up that way."

He walked over to Blitz, unharnessed him from the wagon, and backed it against the curb to keep it from rolling down the icy hill. Blitz lay still, exhausted and trembling.

"Get an old blanket or something out of that junk wagon of yours," the man said, "and put it under his feet so he can get a footing on the ice."

Angry as he was, Joe knew the man was right. He fished around in the wagon, found some old burlap bags, and helped the stranger spread them under Blitz's hoofs.

Taking Blitz by the bridle, the man pulled steadily. "Up, boy," he said gently. "One more try now, and up you go."

Encouraged by the kind voice and steadying pull on his bridle, Blitz made one more effort. This time, his hoofs took hold on the rough burlap and he scrambled to his feet. He stood there, still trembling, while Joe and the stranger harnessed him to the wagon again.

"You'd better take it easy on this ice," the man said to Joe and, giving Blitz a pat on the nose, he walked on down the street.

Joe climbed back on the wagon and took up the reins, but Blitz stood still, afraid of falling if he moved. A new rage swept over Joe. He'd never get home and in out of the storm and cold this way! He jumped off the wagon and, grabbing Blitz by the bridle, he beat him with the steel-bound handle of the whip. Again and again it struck Blitz's aching sides. Blitz cringed in fear and pain, but Joe went on beating him stupidly in his rage.

In that terrible moment, Blitz's heart suddenly turned black inside him and his fear turned to hate against this man. Harking back to his wild ancestors of the plains, he reared and struck at Joe with his forefeet, reaching with bared teeth to bite at the same time. He was fighting as a wild bronco fights in desperation, for its life.

Joe ducked quickly, surprised and frightened. Then rage swept over him again and, standing out of Blitz's reach, he lashed him mercilessly.

"I'll show you who's boss around here, you ugly vicious brute!" he shouted through clenched teeth.

Blitz tried to go on fighting back, but each time he reared and struck out he nearly fell on the bare ice. Finally he stood still and his spirit died within him as he stood. He was numb with pain and fear and hopelessness. He stood with his head hanging, hardly feeling the lash any more.

When Joe saw that Blitz had given in, his anger began to pass. He climbed back on the wagon and took up the reins again.

"Giddap!" he shouted, and Blitz struggled forward in a daze, trying only to keep his feet under him on the ice as he hauled the heavy load up the hill.

Dave Burns Buys
a Horse

SPRING CAME AT LAST, and the ice and cold were gone. Joe hauled his last load of junk and went back to selling flowers. The loads were lighter and the streets no longer slippery, but no one who had known Blitz in his earlier years would have recognized him.

His dirty winter coat was shedding off in ragged patches, showing gaunt ribs and the scars of the whip. His head hung tiredly, except when he jerked back in sudden fear if anyone came close to him. There was a wild look in his eyes, and he laid back his ears and snapped meanly at people who passed near him on the sidewalk. He pulled the wagon as fast as he could, forcing his aching legs to move despite the pain, but he lived in terror of all people and of the whip.

Once a small boy ran up to pat him, saying, "Nice horsey," but his mother dragged him away from Blitz quickly.

"Look out for that vicious horse, Billy!" she cried. "You'll get bitten!"

The little boy looked at Blitz's wild eyes and began to cry with fright.

Another day a woman stopped and spoke kindly to him. Blitz jerked his head away wildly, laying back his ears. The woman stepped back quickly and stood looking at him.

"Poor fellow," she said softly after a minute. "I guess you've really had it rough!"

She turned slowly and walked off down the street. Blitz turned his head and watched her go. These were the first kind words he'd heard in many months and a faint, almost forgotten warmth stirred in his heart. But in a moment it was gone again, and the fear and hopelessness came back.

The months went on. Spring turned to summer, and the city streets became a sweltering nightmare of heat. The scorching sun beat down on Blitz's aching back and he could hardly breathe. Often he stumbled and almost fell, but Joe only jerked viciously on the reins and brought the whip down on his back.

Blitz was slowly starving to death. He ate the scant wisps of mildewed hay Joe gave him, but it wasn't enough to nourish him, and he grew steadily weaker as the months went by. The weaker Blitz grew, the more Joe used the whip to keep him going. Sometimes, in desperation, Blitz snapped or kicked when Joe came to harness him, but it was no use. Joe only struck him with his fist to make him stand still.

By September Blitz was so weak he could hardly pull the wagon at all. He struggled and stumbled blindly through that month, then Joe decided to sell him at the next Fair. Never again would he waste good money on a horse that looked nice but wasn't sound. Next time he'd buy an old plug that was used to poor food and had no spirit to fight back. His old mare had been like that, and she had served him well for five years before she dropped dead in the street. The thirty dollars he'd paid for her had been well spent. He'd buy another one like that.

When the Fair came in October, Joe led Blitz out of the dirty, leaky shed and harnessed him to the wagon for the last time. On the main road, Joe headed Blitz away from the city.

"I'll soon be rid of you now," Joe muttered angrily, bringing the whip down to keep Blitz moving.

The Fair was gay and crowded as usual. The band played and the crowds milled about, looking at all the sideshows and exhibits. Blitz cringed in the far corner of the auction paddock while Joe shouted to everyone who passed to come and look at a good horse, cheap. It was the same wheedling voice with which he sold wilted flowers for more than they were worth. Several people stopped to look, but they didn't stop long. No one came close. Blitz's wild eyes and laid-back ears were enough to warn anyone.

Then out of the crowd came Dr. Burns and his son David. For a long time Dave had been teasing his father to take him to the Fair. Dr. Burns loved his son, and felt bad that he had so little free time to spend with him. A doctor, being on call day and night, does not have an easy life; but whenever something really special came along, Dr. Burns tried to take a few hours off to go with his son.

David looked forward enormously to these rare expeditions with his father. All summer he had mowed lawns and done odd jobs, and he had saved up five dollars to spend when the Fair came to town. The money was in his pocket now, and Dave knew just what he wanted to buy with it.

First of all, he wanted a real bow and some arrows, handmade by an old Indian who sold them every year at the Fair. His friend Peter had bought one there last year and was becoming a really good marksman with it.

Next, Dave wanted a football, so he could practice kicks and runs in the back meadow and get really good at it. He had dreamed long of these things and worked hard for them. Now they would soon be his!

As Dave and his father entered the fairgrounds, they saw the auction paddock filled with horses and ponies. They both loved horses, and Dave had always wanted a pony.

"Dad, couldn't we look at the horses and ponies first?" Dave asked excitedly. After all, this was Dave's first trip to the Fair and he didn't want to miss anything!

"O.K., son," his father said enthusiastically.

"We'll see everything they've got, and we might as well start here."

They wandered into the auction paddock and began looking the horses over. There were all kinds — slim saddle horses, great farm teams with bulging muscles, and, best of all, ponies. Dave looked longingly at the ponies.

"Oh, Dad, how I wish I could have that black and white one!" Dave exclaimed.

"I know, Dave," his father said kindly. "I wish you could too! Maybe someday there'll be enough money to buy one, but not this year, son."

Dave knew that was final and that teasing was no use. He knew there were many things they couldn't afford to have, and Dave had learned to accept this and to enjoy doubly each thing he could have.

Walking reluctantly away from the ponies, they saw Blitz and Joe standing in the corner of the paddock. They stopped and looked, shocked by this ragged, vicious-looking horse.

"Dad, look at that awful old horse," Dave cried. "Gosh, he looks mean!"

"He certainly does," Dr. Burns replied. "He may have been a good horse once, but he's been badly treated. Horses aren't often born mean. They usually get that way from bad treatment. He looks half starved, too, poor beast!"

They turned away, paying no attention to Joe's hopeful shout for them to "come and see a good horse, cheap." As they went out the paddock gate, the auctioneer announced that the bidding was about to begin. A sudden idea came to Dave.

"Dad," he said excitedly, "couldn't we stay and watch the auction and see how much the ponies cost? Then I'd know, and I could work hard and maybe earn enough to buy one next year!"

Dave's father was always glad at his son's willingness to work for things he wanted. He never teased aimlessly like some spoiled kids. If he wanted something badly and his father couldn't afford it, he was glad to work for it. It had been like that about the bow and arrows and the football. All summer Dave had worked for them, and Dr. Burns was proud of his son's efforts.

"That's a good idea, Dave," his father agreed. "I'm afraid they cost much more than you could earn in a year. It will take two anyway. But I'll tell you what I'll do, Dave. If you can earn half the amount thy cost, I'll try to put up the other half!"

"Oh, Dad, how wonderful!" Dave squealed with

excitement. "I'll give up the football and the bow and arrows, and save my five dollars toward a pony!"

They found a place on one of the plank benches and waited for the ponies to be led out. It was a long wait, for the ponies were next to last. One went for a hundred dollars, one for seventy-five, and one for fifty. The black and white one cost most, but the fifty-dollar one looked pretty good. David's excitement was terrific.

"Fifty dollars isn't too bad, Dad," he cried. "I'd only have to earn twenty, because I already have five. If I shovel snow all winter and run errands after school, and then work next summer, I'm sure I can do it, Dad!"

"I think you can too, Dave. It's a deal. I'll start saving the other twenty-five right away," Dave's father said excitedly.

They started to get up to leave, but sudden laughter from the crowd made them look back into the paddock. Joe was battling with Blitz, trying to lead him forward. Blitz was dragging back on the rope, snapping and kicking, his eyes wild.

"Oh, Dad, there's that poor horse. Let's see who buys him," Dave said, suddenly sad at the sight of Blitz.

They settled back on the bench to watch. Finally Joe got Blitz up near the auctioneer's stand, but there were no bids, only laughter from the crowd. Then from the back row a harsh voice shouted:

"Four dollars — for horsemeat!"

Dave was horrified. At first he'd thought it was a little funny, too, about this good-for-nothing old horse. But not for horsemeat. No! The poor old thing. Dave remembered what his father had said —

that he might have been a good horse once, but someone had treated him badly and half starved him, too.

The auctioneer shouted for higher bids, but only laughter answered him. Finally he raised his hammer. "Going — going — g——"

Dave couldn't bear it. Not for horsemeat, that poor old thing! He forgot everything, even the pony. Hardly knowing what he did, Dave jumped to his feet and shouted, "Five dollars!"

A Time of Fear

When David shouted his bid, the crowd laughed again. This was more of a show than they had expected. Even the auctioneer laughed this time. He raised his hammer and shouted to the crowd, "Who will bid higher to save the kid from this vicious bag of bones?"

The crowd jeered, but nobody raised the bid.

"Going — going — GONE, to the boy with five dollars," yelled the auctioneer, and the hammer fell with a sharp thud on the block.

For a minute, Dave's father said nothing. He was proud of the quick kindness in his son that had made him part with that precious five dollars. And he too was sorry for this wretched horse. Nothing to do now but see what could be done with him. He decided to back his son in that effort.

"Well, Dave," he said finally, "it looks as if the horse is yours. We'd better go and see what you've got us into now!"

David's feelings were whirling inside him. Why had he done this thing? His five dollars toward a good pony were gone, and this mean-looking, ragged horse was his instead. But Dave was no quitter. He'd saved the horse from the horsemeat man and he wasn't going to go back on that now.

They walked over to Joe, and Dave handed him the five dollars he had worked so hard to earn. Joe took it reluctantly, disappointed at getting so little for his horse. At least he was rid of him now, and that was some comfort.

"What's his name?" Dave asked.

"His name's Blitz," Joe said. "Means fast as lightning, they say. He's worth a lot more than five dollars. You sure got a buy this time!" Joe added, his old sales talk coming back to him from force of habit.

Dave stepped forward to take the lead rope from Joe's hand, but Blitz plunged back, eyes wild, ears laid back. David was frightened, but he made another try. Then David forgot everything but Blitz. He had seen the quick, wild flash of fear in his eyes, and Dave understood. His father was right about this horse. He wasn't really mean at heart, just terrified. David's heart went out to Blitz in a rush of love and understanding. He began talking to him softly, pleadingly, all his heart in his voice.

"Please, Blitz," he said softly, "please don't be afraid. We only want to save you from the horse-meat man. No one will hurt you any more."

Blitz stood still, trembling all over, and Dave went on talking softly, pleadingly. Blitz pricked one ear forward to listen, then the other ear. He stood transfixed, listening, but still ready for quick defense.

As he listened, a faint, faint memory stirred in Blitz's bewildered brain. A green hillside in the sun, long ago, and a boy like this one reaching out to stroke his nose. As Dave went on talking, the memory grew and spread. The pasture in summer, the warm shadowy barn in winter. Kindness, and the warm feeling of trust in his heart. It was a long time now since Blitz had known these things. Blitz gave a sudden little sobbing sigh and, reaching out his nose, he touched Dave's hand softly. Dave stroked it and Blitz didn't move. There was a murmur of amazement from the crowd. Quietly, Dave took the rope from Joe's hand.

"Come, Blitz," he said. "We're going home. Dad and I will be good to you. Come."

Blitz took a hesitant step forward, and in a minute he was following Dave and his father out of the paddock and down the path to the road.

The silent crowd turned to watch them go — a man, a boy, and a bony, good-for-nothing horse. But instead of the wild, vicious animal that had come into the paddock that morning, they saw only a worn-out, tired nag, his head and tail drooping as he walked quietly beside the boy.

Blitz walked along the road in a daze. He didn't know where they were going or what lay ahead. He had walked down the road from the Fair before, and there was little hope left in his tired heart. He only knew that there was kindness in Dave's voice and in the gentle touch of his hands. He gave another little sobbing sigh and moved closer, his nose touching Dave's arm as they walked along.

"Dad," Dave asked, "can we keep Blitz always, so he'll never be badly treated again?"

"I think so, son," Dr. Burns answered. "I think

he'll be all right with time and kindness, and lots of food and rest. We'll just have to see. But remember, Dave, that Blitz could still be dangerous if anything frightens him suddenly. He's evidently been badly treated for a long time, and it will take time to win his trust again. Remember that, because he might hurt you without meaning to."

"I sure will, Dad," Dave promised, and they walked on down the road toward home.

When they got there, they led Blitz into the old barn behind the house, where Dr. Burns kept his car. They put him in the box stall in the corner and brought him a pail of water. He drank it thirstily.

Dave's mother came out to the barn to see what they were up to now. She hadn't seen them come in but heard their voices in the barn, and she well knew that when they went off together there was no telling what they'd come back with! She looked into the box stall and saw Blitz's bony hulk.

"John!" she cried. "Where did you and Dave get that dreadful horse, and what on earth are you going to do with him?"

"He's not a dreadful horse," Dave said indignantly before his father had time to answer. "He's a poor horse that was badly treated, and I bought him at the Fair to save him from the horsemeat man. Please can I keep him, Ma? Dad says I can!"

"Well, if your Dad says so, Dave. I suppose you can," she answered doubtfully.

Mary Burns had a soft heart too, and an inner fondness for the unlikely projects her husband and son were always getting into together. She never knew what next, but certainly this was the worst project yet. Dr. Burns smiled fondly at her.

"Mary, what are we going to feed this starving beast?" he asked quickly. He knew from long experience that the best way to enlist his wife in any project was to put such a problem up to her.

"Why, we'll call up the feed store right off, John," she answered. "He'll need oats and hay, and a bale of straw for bedding. He can't stand on that hard bare floor! Dave, while I telephone, you take the sickle and cut some of the tall grass behind the barn for him. He needs something to eat right off!"

Dave and his father both came out of the stall and hugged her. Even though this was the worst project they'd got into, Mary Burns was as usual more than equal to it, and all on their side. She laughed and kissed them both.

"John," she said, "there are three calls for you. I

wrote them on the pad in your office. You'll just have time before lunch. Dave and I will take care of the horse while you go."

They went out and left Blitz alone in the stall. He stood peering doubtfully after them. A small spark of warmth and hope had kindled in his tired heart, but he wondered if this too would end, and there would be kicks and the whip again. His head drooped and he sighed wearily.

A New Life Begins

IN A FEW MINUTES, Dave came back into the barn with his arms full of freshly cut grass. He reached out to open the stall door, forgetting his father's warning to move slowly and not startle Blitz. Blitz jumped back as the door opened, his eyes wild again. Dave stopped and spoke gently to him.

"Easy, boy," he said. "Don't be frightened any more. Here's good fresh grass to make you strong and fat."

Blitz quieted, but still stood hesitantly in the far corner of the stall. Dave held out a handful of grass and walked slowly toward him. Blitz was fighting the fear he couldn't help as Dave moved toward him. He was trembling all over again.

Dave stopped and held the grass out to him. It smelled good, and Blitz was starved. Slowly he reached out and took a mouthful. In a few minutes he was munching hungrily on the armful of grass while Dave stroked his neck, and for the first time in many, many months Blitz gave a little nicker of gratitude.

The oats and hay and straw came from the feed store after lunch. As soon as Dr. Burns got home from his afternoon visits, he helped Dave bed Blitz down. They spread the clean, fresh straw in a thick layer on the floor of the stall, while Blitz cringed in the far corner, watching them. He still couldn't get over the fear of people moving close to him. It came over him in a sick dread of suddenly being struck.

Dave and his father talked kindly and moved slowly as they worked. When the straw was all spread, Blitz reached down and sniffed it. It had the good smell of sunny fields. For a whole year Blitz had lived in Joe's reeking, filthy shed. He had almost forgotten about clean straw.

Dave brought him another pail of water, and when Blitz had drunk it, put a measure of oats in the feedbox and an armful of hay in the manger. Then Dave and his father stood quietly and watched. Blitz went on sniffing the clean, golden straw for several minutes. Then he raised his head and sniffed the oats. He pricked his ears forward, happier memories stirring again as he smelt these good smells. He stepped forward and buried his nose hungrily in the oats. When they were gone, he turned to the hay and began on that. Suddenly he stopped eating and, reaching out his long gaunt neck, he touched Dave gently with his nose, nickering softly.

Dr. Burns laughed. "If I ever heard a horse say 'Thank you,' that one did. Stay with it, Dave, and you'll have a gentle horse yet. But remember, it will take time, so be careful still. I don't want to have to patch up any broken bones or horse bites!"

Dave remembered most of the time; but whenever he forgot, Blitz reminded him. At any sudden movement he still jumped back, the wild look in his eyes again. Whenever that happened Dave stood still and talked quietly till the sudden storm of fear had passed out of Blitz's heart. As time went on, it happened less and less often. Blitz was learning to love and trust Dave, and Dave loved Blitz with a fierce loyalty and devotion. All thought of ponies had left him. He had a real horse, and though that horse was still ragged and bony and afraid, Dave dreamed of the day when Blitz would be strong and sound again.

Dave and his father built a little paddock on the sunny south side of the barn. When it was finished, they led Blitz out to it. It was the first time he had been out of his stall since the day of the Fair, and Blitz was jumpy and excited. He sniffed the fresh breeze and shied away from every leaf that blew past him.

"Easy, boy," Dave kept saying. "Leaves don't bite!"

When Blitz was safely in the paddock, Dave and his father leaned on the fence and watched him. At first he stood very still in the corner, afraid to move. Then he sniffed the grass and began to look about him. He lifted his head and sniffed the wind; then he began to explore the paddock cautiously, walking around it slowly several times. Suddenly he nickered and tossed his head and, kicking up his heels like a happy colt, he galloped twice around his new domain.

Dave and his father laughed. Blitz acted a lot younger than he looked! When they took him back to his stall that night, Dr. Burns decided to look at his teeth to see how old he really was. Years ago his father had taught him how to tell, showing him the markings and changes in the teeth that show each year of a horse's life. Dr. Burns had wanted to do it before, but he thought Blitz's teeth were a good thing to keep away from for a while.

Very gently he stroked Blitz's nose, and gradually lifted his lips to see the teeth. Blitz tried to wrench away at first, but finally opened his mouth and let Dr. Burns look. He studied them quickly, and then let Blitz go with a pleased exclamation.

"Dave," he said excitely, "it looks as if you really got something for that five dollars of yours. Blitz is only seven years old — a young horse, right in his prime! He surely must have been starved and beaten and sick to look the way he does."

Dave was thrilled. Blitz wasn't an old worn-out horse after all! He was just sick and starved and frightened. Dave could hardly believe the good news.

As the weeks went by, Blitz's gaunt sides began to fill out, and when he had grown gentler and more used to David, Dr. Burns brought home a brush and currycomb one day.

"Time to start polishing up that horse of yours,"

he laughed as he handed them to Dave. "He still looks as if the moths had been eating him."

He warned Dave to brush only his head and neck at first, keeping away from his legs and hindquarters until Blitz got used to it. He went to the barn with Dave the first time, to see how it went. Blitz nickered and stepped forward, and Dave started brushing his head and neck gently. It felt good, and Blitz lowered his head so David could reach the itchy places behind his ears. The dirty, matted hair came out by the handful as Dave brushed, and under it was the shiny red-brown of the new coat that was growing in. The good food he was eating was beginning to show in many ways. When half his neck was sleek and shining, Dave stepped back, hardly believing.

"Look, Dad," he cried. "Blitz is really beautiful under that old dirty hair! I'll bet he's going to be the most beautiful horse in the world when we get him brushed and fattened up!"

Dr. Burns laughed. "He's got a long way to go yet before he breaks any records for beauty. But he certainly looks a whole lot better than he did."

As they went out, Blitz reached his head over the stall door, nickering softly after them.

Saddled and Ready

THROUGH THE WINTER MONTHS that followed, Blitz ate and rested and grew fat. Dave fed him before he went to school in the morning and again when he came home for lunch. In the afternoon, he brushed and curried him and cleaned out the stall.

As Blitz grew less nervous and jumpy, Dave was able to brush more and more of his ragged coat. Blitz loved the gentle scratching of the brush and currycomb. It soothed the itchy places where old dirty hair was matted, and left him feeling clean and cared for, as he used to be. Finally Dave was able to brush even his hindquarters and hind legs without danger of being kicked; and as he brushed him day after day, Blitz's coat changed color and began to shine. The dirty grayish-brown hair disappeared, and the new hair grew in glossy and red-brown and sleek. White hairs still marked the scars of the whiplashes, and they always would, but they grew less and less noticeable.

When spring came that year, Blitz looked and felt like his old self. Dave was so proud of him he nearly burst. He could hardly believe that he'd bought this wonderful horse for five dollars, just because no one else had seen what the trouble was! Dave laughed to himself when he remembered how much he had wanted to save that five dollars toward a pony instead. Dave was twelve. Soon he would be too big to ride a pony, but he could ride Blitz even when he was grown up. But Dave had not yet ridden Blitz. He often asked his father how soon he could try that, but Dr. Burns kept putting it off.

"Wait, Dave, till Blitz really trusts you. If you try too soon, it will only frighten him and make him hard to handle," he said.

So Dave waited, trying to be patient.

The day school closed for the summer, Dr. Burns drove into the yard as Dave was coming out of the barn. Dave ran to meet him.

"Hi, Dave," Dr. Burns called from the car. "I've got kind of a surprise here for you!"

Dave ran to the car and looked in. On the back seat were a Western saddle and bridle!

"Oh, Dad, how wonderful!" Dave shouted in excitement. "Where did you get them?"

"Well, son," Dr. Burns answered, smiling, "all my patients have heard how you rescued Blitz from the horsemeat man, and they always ask how you and Blitz are getting along. Today, up at the Jones farm, I said I guessed you'd be riding him soon now if we could find a saddle and bridle for sale cheap. Old man Jones said he had an old saddle lying round the barn somewhere, so we went out to look and there it was, hanging in the feed room with the bridle beside it. I wanted to buy it, but he wouldn't hear of it. Said he wanted you to have it as a present from him. So there it is; and as soon as you can ride Blitz, you'd better ride up there and thank him. The old folks would like to see you and Blitz both. They're mighty interested."

"Dad, how wonderful of them!" Dave squealed with excitement. "Can we try it on Blitz now and see if he minds?"

"Sure thing, Dave, but it may take time before

you can ride him safely," Dr. Burns said. "You've found out what patience and going slowly can do. Don't get impatient now and spoil it all."

Dave knew his father was right. It was awfully hard to be patient over anything as exciting as this, but Dave calmed down.

Blitz nickered a greeting as they came in the door, but when they carried the saddle and bridle into the stall, he backed away nervously. It was a long time since he'd worn either saddle or harness, and his memories of harness were still terrifying.

Dave stood still and talked softly to him, and gradually Blitz quieted down. When he was quiet, Dr. Burns showed Dave how to put the bridle on. It was slow, because Blitz kept jerking his head away suddenly, but finally it was on. Blitz chewed nervously on the bit for a few minutes and then got used to it and stuck his nose out for Dave to stroke.

"Good boy!" Dave said softly. "Now we'll put the saddle on, so stand still and don't be frightened."

Blitz tried not to be frightened, but he couldn't seem to help edging away. Dr. Burns lifted the saddle gently onto his back while Dave held the bridle.

"Easy, Blitz," he kept saying softly. "That's only a saddle; it isn't going to hurt you."

Blitz quieted and stood still while Dr. Burns fastened the girth. When the saddle was on, Dave looked at his father with the all-important question in his eyes. Dr. Burns laughed.

"You look mighty anxious to get on this horse!"

"Can I?" Dave pleaded.

"Let's lead him outdoors first and see how he does with just the saddle," Dr. Burns suggested.

They led Blitz out into the sunshine. He tossed his head and was jumpy at first, but he soon got used to the saddle. After all, he'd been ridden many, many times before he fell into bad hands. As the memory of those days came back, he remembered also the laws of a well-trained horse: "Never fight harness, go steadily under the saddle or pulling a wagon. Time enough to frolic when you're not working."

Blitz calmed down again and began to feel very responsible about the whole thing. It was evident that Dave wanted to ride him, and Blitz knew it was up to him to take him safely wherever he wanted to go. He stood very still, as he'd been taught many years ago, waiting for Dave to climb into the saddle.

A Fire Horse
Once and Always

DAVID HAD RIDDEN MANY TIMES BEFORE, and he was a good rider. Bob Peterson, who lived down the road, had a pony and had often let David ride it. So when Dave's father told Dave he could get on Blitz's back, he was not afraid. Blitz was bigger than the pony, but Dave trusted him completely. He climbed up while his father held the bridle. Once in the saddle, Dave waited to see what Blitz would do, but Blitz just tossed his head a little and stood still.

"It looks as if he's going to be all right," Dr. Burns said. "He's evidently used to being ridden, but we don't know much more than that. I'll lead him out to the paddock and you can try him out there till you get used to each other."

Once inside the paddock, Dr. Burns let go of Blitz's bridle and stood back to see what would happen. Blitz stood very still, not sure if he was supposed to move yet. Finally Dave said, "Geddup," and Blitz started off at a careful walk.

"It looks as if he isn't going to run any chances of spilling you off," Dr. Burns laughed. "I hope he always remembers that!"

After Blitz had walked around the paddock several times, Dave gave him a nudge with his heels to make him go faster. Blitz tossed his head and broke into a gentle trot, going around and around the paddock while Dr. Burns watched, smiling.

"Dad, could I try galloping?" Dave shouted. "He goes fine at a trot."

"O.K., son," Dr. Burns called back. "Give it a try."

Dave leaned forward in the saddle and spoke softly to Blitz. "Come on, boy, come on and gallop!"

Blitz eased quickly into a gallop. This was really fun! The sun shone, and the grass was green, and

Blitz was strong and full of spirits again. As he galloped round and round the paddock with Dave on his back, all the happiest memories of his life came back to him. His neck arched proudly, and his silky black tail blew out behind him. He was indeed a handsome horse!

After that, Dave rode him every day. At first in the paddock with Dr. Burns watching, in case anything went wrong. Then Dr. Burns said they could try the road. It was a wonderful summer for both Blitz and Dave. They went farther and farther every day, and sometimes Dave's mother packed him a

picnic lunch to take with him. Blitz grew steadily
stronger, and his stiff joints became limber again.
No one would have guessed that only nine months
before he had been a bony, vicious wreck of a horse.

One day, as Dave and Blitz were trotting down
the village street, the fire alarm blew. Instantly
Blitz was quivering with excitement. Dave thought
he was frightened and tried to reassure him, but
Blitz had other plans. He was off like a shot for the
Fire Station. As the engines roared out into the
street, sirens going and bells clanging, Blitz was
close behind them at the dead gallop.

For a moment Dave thought Blitz was running away. Then he realized that Blitz was following the engines instead of running away from them; and forgetting his own fright, Dave leaned forward in the saddle, urging him on. But Blitz needed no urging. Fast as the motorized engines were, Blitz kept close behind them. The firemen on the last engine, seeing the boy and horse following them at breakneck pace, began to laugh and cheer them on. It was more fun than Dave had ever had!

A mile out from the village, the engines turned in at a farm, with Blitz and Dave still following. The fire, in a tool shed near the barn, was quickly put out. As soon as it was safely out, the firemen came over to look at the horse who had raced them to the fire.

"That's some fast horse you have, Dave!" the Fire Chief said. "How'd you get him to go so fast?"

"I didn't," Dave said. "He just went by himself as soon as he heard the first fire whistle blow."

The Fire Chief scratched his head. He'd been in the Fire Department for years, and many a fast fire horse had he driven in his day. He looked Blitz over again, noticing the excited glint in his eyes and the strong chest and legs.

"What's his name?" the Fire Chief asked.

"Blitz," Dave said.

The Fire Chief thought for a minute, trying to remember where he'd heard that name before. Suddenly it came to him. The famous red-bay horse of the Drumlin Fire Department had been called Blitz. Everyone in the county had heard of that horse! They had also heard of the terrible accident, and how Blitz had finally been sold, good for light work only.

"So that's the horse you bought at the Fair and nursed back to health?" the Fire Chief asked.

"That's right," Dave said. "I paid five dollars for him."

The firemen laughed. "You certainly got a buy that time!" they said.

The Fire Chief told Dave that Blitz must be the famous Drumlin fire horse who had been injured in a bad accident two years before.

"Judging by the shape he was in when you got him," he said, "he must have fallen into mighty bad hands when Sye Perkins sold him. I'm sure glad you rescued him. Terrible to see a fine horse like that abused."

Dave was thrilled. Blitz had been a real fire

horse! Now he knew where Blitz had come from, and why he had turned out so wonderfully with kindness and good food and rest.

"I'm sure glad I got him!" Dave exclaimed.

"I'll bet you are." the Fire Chief said. "I must write to Sye Perkins and tell him what's become of his horse. He'll be mighty glad to hear what a good home he has now. I hear Sye was pretty smashed up in that accident, too, but he's back in the Fire Department now, driving the new truck. Once a fireman, always a fireman, I guess."

Dave could hardly wait to get home and tell his father about Blitz's past as a fire horse. They galloped home, and Dave poured out the exciting news.

After that, Dave and Blitz never missed a fire. Wherever they were when the whistle blew, Blitz wheeled around and dashed for the Fire Station. Then the mad race with engines was on. It was hard to tell who loved it most, Blitz or Dave!

A Sick Call
for Dr. Burns

W HEN FALL CAME, Dave went back to school and there was less time for riding. But after school, he saddled Blitz for a short ride at least, before the early winter darkness set in. The weekends were free for longer excursions. After the first snow, Dave rode Blitz to the blacksmith's and had sharp pegs put on his shoes to keep him from slipping. At Christmas, Dave found a pair of cowboy boots and a brand new bridle for Blitz under the Christmas tree. He was wild with excitement!

Pulling on the boots as fast as he could, he dashed out to the barn to show Blitz the bridle. Blitz nickered and sniffed it with interest and Dave pulled off the halter and tried it on. It was really beautiful. Its soft strong leather was decorated with shiny silver studs that glittered as Blitz tossed his head. Dave was entranced! Although it was snowing hard, Dave was too excited to wait for a little thing like good weather and, saddling Blitz, he galloped into the village to show off the new boots and bridle.

There was heavy snow that winter, and the town plows were kept busy. But in January the great blizzard struck, the worst storm in twenty years.

By noon the sky was already black, and a low moaning wind swept up the valley, carrying the snow with it. The schools closed for the day, and by two o'clock in the afternoon all the stores in the town had closed too. Everyone hurried to get home before the driving snow blocked the roads completely. The plows worked desperately, but the snow was too much for them.

Dave got home at twelve thirty and ran out to the barn to feed Blitz. He piled some extra straw in the stall to keep him warm, then ran into the house to have lunch with his mother.

Dr. Burns skipped lunch altogether and stayed out, trying to get to every patient who needed him before the storm blocked the roads. He got home at three o'clock, cold and hungry. His was the last car off the road, but he had finished his calls and had seen that every patient was taken care of. He drove his car into the barn, stopped to give Blitz a friendly pat, then closed and fastened the barn door against the wind. He went into the kitchen, stamping the snow off his boots and shedding his snow-covered coat as he went.

"Looks like a humdinger this time!" he said, kissing his wife and giving Dave an affectionate slap on the back. "But I got my work finished and, short of an emergency, it looks as if I'll get the rest of the day off. Here's hoping there won't be any emergencies before morning!"

All afternoon the blizzard roared around the house. By nightfall the town was completely snowed in. Great white drifts lay across the roads, and although the plows were still working steadily, they couldn't keep up with it. Not a car could move, even in the center of the town.

As night settled in, the whistling of the wind grew wilder, the bare tree trunks groaning as they bent before it. Dave and his father and mother ate their supper by the fireplace in the sitting room.

The old furnace was going full blast, but the icy wind seeped in through every small crack around windows and doors. Dr. Burns piled logs on the crackling fire, making a cozy circle of warmth against the storm.

After supper, Dave brought out a ship model he was making, and his father helped him work on it. His mother brought out the socks to darn, and they talked and laughed as they worked. It wasn't often that they had a quiet evening together. Usually Dr. Burns was out on a round of calls and Dave had to study his lessons for school. But it was a safe guess there'd be no school tomorrow, and Dr. Burns couldn't have gotten his car out if he'd wanted to. Dave sat up till ten o'clock that night, and before he went to bed Mrs. Burns made hot chocolate for them all. It was a wonderful evening despite the storm.

When Dave finally did go to bed, he couldn't sleep. He lay in his warm bed, listening to the howling wind outside. The whole house shook, and it seemed as if it would blow down in the roaring blast. Dave could hear the snow clicking against the window panes, a barrage of tiny icy particles coming in fierce gusts with the wind. He had left the door of his room open, and he could hear his mother and father still talking and laughing downstairs. The sound came to him faintly, almost drowned out by the roar of the storm. It was a happy, comforting sound.

It was almost midnight when Dave heard the faint tinkling of the telephone in the hall at the foot of the stairs. He heard his father answer it, and although he couldn't hear what was said, he heard the sudden concern that came into his father's voice. He jumped out of bed and ran to the top of the stairs.

"What is it, Dad?" he called as his father hung up the receiver.

Dr. Burns looked up the stairs at Dave's shivering figure at the top.

"It's about the little Olsen girl, son," he called. "Deathly sick, and no way for me to get out to their farm tonight! I've got to get there somehow — but how?"

Dave ran down the stairs and followed his father back to the fireplace. This was no night for sleeping, and his father let him come. After all, it was just as well for Dave to learn what a doctor's life was like, for already Dave was determined to be a doctor when he grew up.

"What is it, John?" Dave's mother asked anxiously.

Dr. Burns told her. The little Olsen girl had gone to school with a bad sore throat. She'd walked home in the storm; and when she got there, she was chilled to the bone. Toward evening fever set in. The Olsens had done everything they could, but her fever was going steadily up. It was 105 degrees when they called, and she could hardly breathe!

Dave's mother looked at her husband with deep anxiety. "That dear little Olsen girl!" she exclaimed. "But John, you can't even get the car out of the barn. Every road is blocked for miles around."

"I know, I know," Dr. Burns agreed, "but somehow I've got to get there! The question is *how*. I've got my skis. It will be mighty slow going in this wind, but at least there'll be a chance of getting there. It sounds like diphtheria to me, and I can't just sit here and let the child die.

"If only there were a faster way than skis!" he said, pacing up and down the floor.

When Dave's father said the word "fast," an idea burst into Dave's head.

"Dad," he cried excitedly, "why don't you go on

Blitz? He's fast and strong. He'll get you there!"
Dr. Burns whirled around and faced his son. He
saw Dave's face, torn between anxiety and excitement, and in his eye he saw the glint of courage and
determination that he was proud to see. For Dave,
too, the one thought was to get there and save that
child, and he was willing to risk both his father and
his beloved horse toward that end!

"You've struck it, son," he said proudly. "Blitz
is the answer! Why didn't I think of it myself?"

Dr. Burns gave Dave a hug and bolted for his office to get the antitoxin and medicines he'd need.
His wife ran to the kitchen to make sandwiches and
a Thermos bottle of hot coffee for him to take. Dave
ran to his room to get the old leather saddlebag
that fastened behind Blitz's saddle. It would be just
the thing for his dad's medical kit!

Dr. Burns packed his medical kit in the saddlebag and pulled on his warm boots and heavy storm
coat, while Dave and his mother packed the sandwiches and coffee in the saddlebag beside the kit.
Dave wanted to get dressed and help his father saddle Blitz, but Dr. Burns said there wasn't time. He
kissed his wife an affectionate good-bye, then laid
his hand gently on Dave's shoulder.

111

"Take good care of your mother, Dave, till I get back," he said softly.

He swung the saddlebag over his shoulder, took the lantern in his hand, and opened the kitchen door. An icy blast of wind and snow swept into the kitchen as Dr. Burns stepped out into the storm and the darkness, closing the door behind him.

Through the Blizzard

D<small>R</small>. B<small>URNS</small> <small>FOUGHT</small> <small>HIS</small> <small>WAY</small> through the drifts to the barn. He could hardly stand up in the fierce wind, and the snow blew in blinding gusts in his face. Instead of trying to open the big barn door, which was half buried by snow, he went to the small side door in the lee of the barn. In a minute he was inside and heard Blitz's nicker of welcome. Blitz had been dozing restlessly as the old beams of the barn creaked and groaned in the roaring wind. He was very glad to see Dave's father.

"You and I are in for a night of it, old boy!" Dr. Burns said, as he lifted the saddle quickly onto

Blitz's back. "I'm counting on you to get me there, Blitz, storm or no storm!"

Blitz didn't know where they were going, or why, but he sensed the urgency in Dr. Burns's voice. The same feeling of excitement came over him that he had felt when the Drumlin fire whistle used to blow in the night. In a second he was wide awake and raring to go. He tossed his head and snorted with impatience. As soon as Blitz was saddled, Dr. Burns led him out into the roaring gale. He closed the barn door, swung up onto Blitz's back, and they were off!

As he rode past the house, Dr. Burns saw his wife and Dave waving as they watched him go. He waved back. Then, in a moment, they were swallowed up in the darkness and the swirling snow.

Blitz soon found that this was no galloping job. The drifts were up to his chest, and it took all the strength of his powerful muscles to plunge his way through them. Often he had to rear and leap into them, one jump at a time, to break through at all. The wind lashed at him and the flying snow half blinded him. Dr. Burns leaned over his neck, guiding him the best he could and urging him on. The lantern only threw its light a few feet into the thick whirling snow. For a minute Dr. Burns wondered how they would ever find the way, but as they reached the road, they brushed past a telephone pole.

"That's it, old boy!" Dr. Burns shouted above the gale. "The telephone poles run all the way to the Olsen farm. I'll keep the light on the poles. You'll have to do the rest!"

Blitz nickered and plunged harder than ever into the drifts. He was sweating already, despite the icy cold, and it was hard to breathe. The wind seemed to blow his breath back down his throat!

One telephone pole — two telephone poles — three telephone poles. It seemed as if it had taken an hour to get past three of them! It was a mile and a half to the Olsen farm. Would Blitz's strength hold out that long? Dr. Burns prayed silently that it would. If Blitz failed, the Olsen child would die, and probably he and Blitz would die too, lost in the raging storm!

Blitz was panting already, and every little while Dr. Burns pulled him to a stop and turned him tail to the wind, to rest and get his breath. The snow was growing deeper every minute, and each step was harder than the last.

"On, boy," Dr. Burns urged. "We've got to make it!"

Blitz struggled on. Finally they reached the wooden bridge over the creek and Dr. Burns shouted with excitement.

"Only half a mile more, Blitz! Stay with it, boy. Easy does it, easy and steady. Save your strength as much as you can. You'll need all you've got!"

Blitz nickered in answer. Every muscle in him ached with exhaustion, and his breath came in hurting gasps against the icy wind, but he struggled on and on. He had no thought of quitting. Wherever Dr. Burns was going, Blitz aimed to get him there.

But Blitz and Dr. Burns were not there yet! On the far side of the bridge, Blitz fell in a drift-covered ditch. Dr. Burns was thrown into the deep snow beside him, and for a moment they both lay still, too exhausted to move. Then Blitz struggled to get up, but he couldn't get his feet under him in the deep snow.

Dr. Burns lifted his head. He was so terribly cold and tired! He wanted to just lie there and not bother to move, but he knew that deep drowsiness was the beginning of freezing to death. He must fight it off somehow!

He battled with the snow and got to his feet. Blitz was lying beside him, his flanks heaving and his breath coming in short, hard gasps.

"Blitz, boy," Dr. Burns shouted, "you've got to get up. Up boy! We're almost there! We can't give up now, either of us!"

Blitz heard and struggled again. Dr. Burns took hold of his bridle and steadied him, and Blitz scrambled to his feet at last. Dr. Burns led him back to the road and turned him tail to the wind to rest for a few minutes, while he reached in the saddlebag for the hot coffee and sandwiches. He fed the sandwiches to Blitz to give him strength, and Blitz ate them with hungry relish and a nicker of gratitude. Dr. Burns drank the steaming coffee. He could feel its warmth spread through his body, thawing the numbness.

When he had finished the coffee, Dr. Burns swung back into the saddle and they faced the storm again. The minutes seemed like hours, and the drifts higher and more impassable than ever as they struggled on. Suddenly a faint light glimmered through the blinding snow!

"Blitz!" Dr. Burns shouted above the wind. "It's the Olsen farm! We're there, boy! We made it! You got me here!"

Blitz nickered faintly. He didn't have enough breath left for any more. A few more plunges, a few more yards, and there was the Olsens' door in front of them.

"Thank God!" Dr. Burns said softly.

"The Very Best Horse in the World"

THE DOOR OPENED just as Dr. Burns swung down off Blitz's back. Dan Olsen had been sitting by the window, staring out into the storm. Dr. Burns had said he would come. Dan didn't see how he could, but there was nothing to do but hope. He'd tried to telephone again, but the wires were down in the storm.

Dan's wife, Saima, was sitting beside their little girl, doing everything she could to make her comfortable. But the fever raged, and the child tossed and turned, hardly able to breathe. Dan had tried to help too, but there was nothing more that he could do. Finally he went to the chair by the window and sat down to wait, praying silently that their little girl would somehow be saved.

Suddenly the ghostly shadow of a man and horse loomed out of the whirling snow outside the window. Dan could hardly believe his eyes. He thought he must be dreaming. No one, man or horse, could get through this storm! But as he looked, the shadow moved forward into the light by the doorstep. It was Blitz and Dr. Burns! Olsen leaped out of his chair and ran to the door. The wind and snow rushed in as he opened it.

"Doc!" he cried. "However did you make it? Bless you, sir, for coming!"

"How's the child?" Dr. Burns asked quickly.

"She's very sick indeed, Doc, terribly sick!" Dan answered. "But now that you're here maybe you can save her!"

"I hope so, Dan," Dr. Burns said. "Look, Dan, Blitz brought me through the storm. He's worn out and he's wringing wet with sweat. Please get him into the barn and do what you can for him."

"You bet I will, Doc!" Dan said, reaching for his coat and boots and, taking the lantern, he led Blitz off to the barn.

Dr. Burns hurried into the house, carrying the saddlebag. Mrs. Olsen ran out into the hall to greet him.

"Oh, Doc," she cried, "how did you ever get here? I never thought you would. Inga is desperately sick!"

Dr. Burns shed his snow-covered coat and boots as quickly as he could and followed Mrs. Olsen into the bedroom, where the little girl lay tossing in the bed.

"There, there, Inga," he said softly, stroking her forehead. "We'll have you right again in no time! Let's have a look at that throat of yours."

Inga opened her eyes and looked up at him, but she was too sick to speak. Dr. Burns opened her mouth and examined her throat.

"It's diphtheria all right," he said, turning to Inga's mother. "We must give the antitoxin at once."

He went to the kitchen and boiled his hypodermic, to sterilize it; then went back to the bedroom and gave Inga the antitoxin. When that was done, he lighted the croup kettle he'd brought with him and held it so that Inga could breathe its soothing steam. He worked steadily over her, doing everything that could be done. Finally he sat down beside the bed, waiting for the antitoxin to do its work. Saima Olsen brought him hot coffee and biscuits while they waited.

Out in the barn Dan Olsen was working over Blitz. He rubbed him dry with handfuls of clean straw, then put a warm horse blanket over him. Blitz stood gratefully in the dry bedding of the stall. His head hung heavily with exhaustion, and his flanks still heaved. Gradually he got his wind back and stood resting quietly. Dan went back to the house, mixed a warm mash, and carried it to the barn. Blitz ate it hungrily and gratefully.

"I guess you're all right now, boy," Dan said softly. "Rest well. You deserve it! I'll bet there isn't another horse in the county that could have got through this storm and brought Dr. Burns to our little girl!"

Giving Blitz a loving pat, Dan left him and battled his way back to the house through the wind and snow. He found Dr. Burns and Saima still sitting anxiously beside little Inga, who lay in a deep sleep after the hours of restless tossing. Her breathing seemed easier and her face less flushed with fever. All three of them sat there beside her while the minutes and hours ticked slowly by. There was nothing to do now but wait, listening to the raging wind outside.

Toward morning the fury of the storm began to die down. The snow had stopped, and the wind came only in brief angry gusts. In the east there was a bright streak of dawn across the sky.

Back at Dr. Burns's house in the village, the clock on the mantelpiece struck seven. David woke up on the sofa by the fire, where he had fallen asleep. His mother was standing by the window, looking out.

"The storm is over, Dave," she said, "but all the wires are down. We must get word to the snow-plows to try to get through to the Olsen farm and find your father!"

"I'll go on my skis and tell them," Dave said, and ran upstairs to get dressed.

In a few minutes Dave was ready and off on his skis, headed for the village. He made good time over the frozen snow, and found the plow crews just ready to start out again. They'd been in for hot coffee and to refuel the plows, having already cleared part of the village streets.

When Dave told them his father had ridden Blitz

to the Olsen farm in the night, the men looked grave.

"In that storm!" the foreman exclaimed. David's anxious face stopped him from saying more and, turning to the plow crews, he shouted, "Well, what in blazes are you standing there gaping for? Get going! Get every plow and every man we've got on the road to the Olsen farm, and fast! And get the ambulance to follow as soon as the road is cleared. It may be needed! For the Olsen girl, of course," he added lamely, catching a glimpse of David's worried face.

Dave wanted terribly to go with the plows to find his father and Blitz, but his father's parting words were still strong in his mind: "Take good care of your mother, Dave, till I get back." So Dave raced home on his skis as the powerful plows roared out into the road, headed for the Olsen farm.

Up at the farm, Dr. Burns was standing beside little Inga's bed, one hand on her pulse. "Her pulse is steadying," he said, "and the fever's dropping fast. We'd better get her to the hospital as soon as the road is cleared, so she'll get the best of care, but I'm sure she's going to be all right. The antitoxin has done a good job!"

"How can we ever thank you enough, Doc, for riding through that storm to save our Inga!" Saima and Dan said in one breath.

"It's Blitz you owe her life to, really," Dr. Burns said. "Without Blitz, I couldn't possibly have got here. We only just made it as it was!"

Suddenly the wintry silence was broken by a distant roar. Dan ran to the window and looked down the valley toward the town.

"It's the plows!" he shouted. "They're coming up the hill, and the ambulance is right behind them."

An hour later the plows roared their way back to the village, the ambulance following on the hard-packed snow in their wake. When they reached Dr. Burns's house, Dave and his mother were already waiting anxiously by the road.

"All's well with everybody!" the foreman yelled above the noise of the engine as the first plow snorted its way past them.

The two other plows went growling by before the ambulance reached the driveway and stopped. Dr. Burns jumped out and hugged his wife and son happily.

"Blitz got me there, and the Olsen girl will live!"

he said, hugging them both again. "The ambulance is taking her to the hospital now."

Dr. Burns's eyes fell on Dave's face, and he saw the silent question in his eyes.

"Yes, Dave," he said, "Blitz is all right too. Dan is leading him down behind his sleigh. Ought to be here any minute now. Blitz is a great horse, Dave. No other horse I ever knew could have made it through that storm. You know, Dave, the best thing you ever did in all your life was saving Blitz from the horsemeat man!"

"I know, Dad," Dave said softly. "I guess Blitz didn't just save Inga Olsen's life. He saved yours too, didn't he, Dad?"

"Yes, son," Dr. Burns answered. "Blitz saved us both. I never could have made it through that storm on skis. It wouldn't have been possible."

They looked up as a gay jingling of sleigh bells rang across the frozen snow. It was Dan Olsen's white horse trotting down the road at a good clip with Dan in the sleigh. Close behind it came Blitz, head up, neck arched, snorting puffs of mist into the frozen air. In a minute they were at the gate and Dave's arms were around Blitz's neck. Blitz nickered happily as Dave's mother and father hugged him too.

"May God bless you all!" Dan Olsen said as Dave untied Blitz's lead rope from the sleigh. "Saima and I will never forget how Blitz brought Dr. Burns through the worst blizzard in twenty years."

Olsen clucked to his horse and the sleigh went jingling off down the road, following the ambulance. When they were out of sight, Dr. Burns and his wife went into the house, while Dave led Blitz proudly to the barn.

"You're the very best horse in all the world!" Dave said, as he put Blitz in the warm straw-bedded stall and gave him an extra big feed of oats. Blitz nuzzled Dave's arm and nickered softly.